Faith
the Cinderella
Fairy

WITHDRAWN

To Lara, with love

Special thanks to Rachel Elliot

Text copyright © 2016 by Rainbow Magic Limited

ISBN 978-0-545-85195-4

10 9 8 7 6 5 4 3 2 1   16 17 18 19 20

Printed in the U.S.A.   40

First edition, January 2016

Faith
the Cinderella
Fairy

by Daisy Meadows

SCHOLASTIC INC.

The Fairyland Palace

Fairy Tale Lane

Rachel's Ho

Tippington Town

Jack Frost's
Ice Castle

Forest

Tiptop Castle

The Fairy Tale Fairies are in for a shock!
Cinderella won't run at the strike of the clock.
No one can stop me—I've plotted and planned,
And I'll be the fairest one in all of the land.

It will take someone handsome and witty and clever
To stop storybook endings forever and ever.
But to see fairies suffer great trouble and strife,
Will make me live happily all of my life!

Contents

A Tiptop Morning

"Another beautiful day at Tiptop Castle!" exclaimed Rachel Walker, throwing open the window and breathing in the crisp morning air.

She was looking out of the bedroom that she was sharing with her best friend, Kirsty Tate. They had been having a fun

time at the Fairy Tale Festival, and
they couldn't wait for this morning's
ballroom-dancing lesson.

"I can't believe how lucky we are,"
said Kirsty, who was brushing her hair at
the beautiful vanity table. "It's amazing
that the festival is being held here, so
close to Tippington—and we've made
some great new friends."

Lots of children were staying at the castle, and there were fun fairy tale activities to enjoy every day. Tippington was Rachel's hometown, and Mrs. Walker had arranged this special treat for them while Kirsty was visiting during spring vacation.

"It was so much fun dressing up yesterday," said Rachel, thinking of their fairy outfits. "I wonder what adventures today will bring!"

"Magical ones, I hope," said Kirsty with a happy smile.

On their first day at the castle, the girls had met their friend Hannah the Happily Ever After Fairy while they were exploring. They had shared many adventures in Fairyland, because they were good friends with the fairies, and

they were thrilled when Hannah
whisked them off to meet some very
special fairies: the seven Fairy Tale
Fairies.

The fairies gave the girls *The Fairies'
Book of Fairy Tales*. It was a wonderful
collection of the girls' favorite fairy tales,
but when they looked inside, the pages
were blank.

Thinking about the fairies' shocked
faces, Rachel felt a pang of worry.

"It would be wonderful to be able to
help another of the Fairy Tale Fairies,"
she said.

Kirsty nodded. Right after the girls
met them, the fairies had discovered that
Jack Frost had stolen their magic objects.
Without them, the characters in their
fairy tales fell out of their stories and got

lost! Jack Frost was planning to rewrite the fairy tales to star him and his goblins, and he had taken the fairies' objects to the human world.

"We should go down to the ballroom," said Kirsty, looking at her alarm clock. "The ballroom-dancing lesson will be starting soon and I don't want to miss a second!"

The girls hurried down the spiral staircase, still thinking about their

fairy friends. So far, they had helped
Julia the Sleeping Beauty Fairy and
Eleanor the Snow White Fairy get their
magic objects back. Now Sleeping
Beauty and her prince and Snow White
and the seven dwarves were all back
inside their worlds. But there were still
five magic objects left to find, and many
more fairy tale characters to return to
their stories.

The best friends ran all the way
through the castle, but Kirsty
paused when
they reached the
ballroom. Rachel
stopped, too.

"Are you OK?" she
asked in concern.

"What if I'm not

good enough?" said Kirsty, sounding suddenly nervous.

"That's why we're having lessons," said Rachel, squeezing her hand. "Anyway, it's just for fun. Don't worry!"

She pushed open the door and stepped inside. The first thing she saw was a young woman standing on a stool, polishing one of the gold-framed mirrors that lined the walls.

"Hello," said Rachel as Kirsty followed

her into the room. "Are we in the right place for the dance lesson?"

The young woman turned and gave them a beautiful smile.

"I think so," she said in a longing voice. "The others are over there—it sounds like lots of fun!"

She waved her rag toward the far end of the ballroom, where a small group of

children were giggling and dancing around.

"Thank you very much," said Rachel, wondering why the young woman wasn't joining in with the lesson.

She and Kirsty went to join the others, and then one of the festival organizers entered the room, dressed in a beautiful silver gown.

"Hello, everyone!" she said. "I'm Rosie, your dance instructor for this morning. I hope that this beautiful ballroom will inspire you to dance like true fairy tale princes and princesses!"

Two Rude Girls

Looking around, Rachel and Kirsty understood exactly what she meant. The grand ballroom had plush velvet curtains at the windows and a huge crystal chandelier hanging from the ceiling.

"Let's start with a waltz," said Rosie. "I'll give you a demonstration first, and then you can try it."

Rosie showed them the whirling waltz steps several times, and then everyone found a partner and started to practice. Rachel and Kirsty danced together. At first they felt as if they were doing really well, but when they tried to twirl, their feet somehow got tangled up. They ended up in a heap on the floor, giggling helplessly.

"That was awful," said a mean, nasal voice.

"Really dreadful," said another voice, sounding even ruder.

Rachel and Kirsty looked up and
saw two girls glaring at them through
narrowed eyes.

They were both
wearing fussy
ball gowns in
bright colors,
and they looked
as if they had
stuck on false
eyelashes—very
badly.

"What strange costumes," said Kirsty
under her breath.

"What bad manners," said Rachel,
scrambling to her feet. "Come on, let's
try those steps again."

"You shouldn't be allowed on the
dance floor," said one of the girls. "Move

out of the way. We'll show you how dancing should be done!"

"Let's go," said Rachel in a low voice.

They moved to the side of the ballroom and watched as the mean girls elbowed their way past other dancers and whirled around,  getting all the steps wrong. Rosie kept stopping them and trying to show them the correct steps, but they didn't want to listen. One by one, the other children in the class came over to stand with Rachel and Kirsty.

"This isn't much fun," said Emily, who was dancing with Aaron. "Let's go and find somewhere else to practice our steps."

Everyone thought this was a very good idea, and they started to leave the ballroom. Rachel and Kirsty were last, and as they went to follow the others, something caught Kirsty's eye. She looked up and saw a fairy fluttering down from the crystal chandelier!

It was Faith the Cinderella Fairy, and she was looking excited.

"Hello, girls!" she
said in a happy
voice.
"Hello!"
said Rachel.
"Does
your smile
mean that
you've found
your magic
object?"

"No," said Faith,
her smile fading slightly. "But I have
found Cinderella!"

"Oh, where is she?" asked Kirsty with
a gasp.

Faith laughed and waved at the young
woman who was still polishing the
framed mirrors and pictures on the walls.

Rachel and Kirsty could hardly believe it—the young woman they had talked to earlier was Cinderella!

Cinderella waved back and Faith let out a little sigh.

"I have to find my magic glass slipper soon," she said. "Without it, Cinderella is stuck here in the human world and her fairy tale is ruined."

Just then, the ballroom door opened and Jack Frost swaggered in, walking in a somewhat lopsided way.

"He's wearing two different shoes," said Rachel in surprise.

"One of them is my shoe," said Faith in a horrified voice. "It's my magic glass slipper, and as long as he's got it, he will be able to do anything he wants with Cinderella's fairy tale."

Rachel glanced over at the mean girls, but they were too busy arguing about steps with Rosie to notice what was going on at the other end of the ballroom.

"You," Jack Frost snapped, pointing an accusing finger at Cinderella. "Come and clean my Ice Castle from top to bottom right now."

"But I have to find my way home and

finish my cleaning," Cinderella pleaded. "If I don't make the house sparkle, my stepmother won't allow me to go to the ball tonight."

"Tough luck," said Jack Frost. "I'm preparing for a fabulous ball myself tonight, and I'm going to be the star of the show. I need a nice clean castle, and you're going to help me!"

"But the ball is all I've dreamed about," cried poor Cinderella, clasping her hands together.

"I couldn't care less," Jack Frost barked at her. "You're coming with me!"

With a bolt of icy magic, Jack Frost and Cinderella vanished back to Fairyland.

"Quick, turn us into fairies!" Kirsty exclaimed. "There's no time to lose!"

Whisked to Fairyland

Faith's wand moved so fast that it was just a blur of sparkles. Instantly, the ballroom disappeared and Rachel and Kirsty were in Fairyland before they had time to catch their breath. They found themselves fluttering on gauzy wings, high above Jack Frost's Ice Castle. It was early evening, and the setting sun shone on the gray stone walls.

"That's funny," said Rachel. "There are usually lots of goblins on guard, but I can't see a single one."

"Let's go and find out what's going on," said Faith.

The three fairies swooped down and entered the castle through an open door. They flew quickly through damp, dripping hallways, shivering in the sudden darkness. Rachel and Kirsty

had been inside the castle before, so they led the way. When they were close to the Throne Room, Kirsty stopped so suddenly that Faith almost bumped into her.

"Listen!" Kirsty said in a low voice. "I think I can hear something."

They paused and heard the bad-tempered squawking voices of several goblins coming from the room opposite the Throne Room.

"Come on," said Faith. "Let's find out what they're shouting about."

The door was open, so it was easy for the three tiny fairies to slip inside without being noticed. They flew up to a high curtain rod, hid behind the fabric, and gazed down upon a wintry ballroom.

Icicle chandeliers hung from the ceiling. Shiny blue and white stars made of ice dangled from them. There were several goblins on their hands and knees, polishing the wooden floor. Others were painting snowflakes on the tall windows and stringing blue lights around some ragged-looking potted plants.

Rachel spotted goblins dressed as chefs, each carrying a platter piled high with green and blue cupcakes. Three goblins were crowded around a small desk, writing invitations very slowly and elbowing each other as they wrote. So far they had only completed the first line:

You are hereby invited to a spectacular ball in honor of a mystery guest.

"Look," Kirsty whispered, nudging Rachel and Faith. "There's Cinderella."

Still wearing her ragged clothes, Cinderella was busily dusting a huge silver throne at the front of the ballroom.

"Poor thing," said Rachel. "How can we help her escape?"

"First we have to find Jack Frost and get my glass slipper back," said Faith. "Then Cinderella will be able to return to her story."

Just then, Kirsty noticed a trail of richly

embroidered clothes scattered across a grand staircase behind the throne.

"I bet Jack Frost made that mess," she said. "He would expect Cinderella or the goblins to clean up for him."

"Let's take a look!" said Rachel, feeling excited.

Staying hidden from the goblins, they flew over to the clothes and fluttered up the staircase. Kirsty saw that Cinderella looked very unhappy and wished they could comfort her, but she knew that they shouldn't risk being seen.

At the top of the stairs, the trail of beautiful clothes led them to a very big walk-in closet. The door was wide open, and a steady line of goblins was walking in with armfuls of puffy, lacy, fancy outfits.

"No, no, NO!" Jack Frost yelled
from inside the room. "My outfit has to
be the best. These are all ugly—take
them away!"

A goblin came flying out of the room
and landed on his bottom. A mound of
pink fabric followed him and fell on his
head. While the other goblins were
laughing, the fairies slipped into the
dressing room and hid behind a curtain.
They found themselves next to a tall
window, which looked down over the
snow-covered forest beside the castle.
Faith peeked through the curtain, and
Rachel and Kirsty peered over her
shoulders.

In the middle of the room, Jack Frost
was standing in front of a big three-
way mirror, frowning at his reflection.

He was wearing green robes and a goblin
was sitting at his feet with a mouthful
of pins.

"What about this one, Your Iciness?"
asked another goblin.

"I told you, you have to call me
Cinderfrost!" Jack Frost yelled. "And
you had better find me the perfect ball
outfit—or else!"

A Moaning
Mystery Guest

Jack Frost tore the robes off and kicked
them away, holding out his hand for
the next outfit. This was pale blue with
white ruffles. He pulled it on with rough
hands, and a goblin tied a yellow sash
around his waist.

"That doesn't match!" Jack Frost howled. "Take it off! Hurry up—you're too slow!"

"He's still wearing my magic glass slipper," Faith said, noticing as Jack aimed a kick at the goblin who had tied the yellow sash.

"How can we get it off his foot?" Kirsty wondered aloud.

Rachel was looking out the window, and noticed two goblins running away from the castle through the snow, each carrying a large mail bag.

"They must be going to deliver the invitations," she murmured.

"This isn't good enough for Cinderfrost!" Jack Frost snarled, drawing Rachel's attention back to the dressing room.

"What about a diamond pendant?" a goblin nervously suggested.

"I know!" Rachel whispered. "We need a pair of shoes that Jack Frost will like better than the magic glass slipper!"

Faith waved her wand at the big wardrobe and a pair of sparkly ice-blue shoes appeared. A goblin grabbed them.

"Look, these are blue like the beautiful robes," he squeaked. "They're just the thing!"

The goblins gathered around in admiration as Jack put on one of the sparkly shoes.

"A perfect fit!" said one.

"Fabulous!" said another. "Put on the other one!"

The fairies leaned forward, keeping their fingers crossed. But Jack Frost shook his head.

"I'm not taking off this glass slipper," he snapped.

The goblin at his feet frowned.

"But it's too big," he argued. "The sparkly ones look much better."

"I'll just wear one of each," Jack Frost declared.

The goblins started to laugh, and Jack Frost glowered at them.

"You're no help at all!" he shouted. "I need a fairy godmother to help me dress for the ball."

He stamped the foot that was wearing the magic glass slipper, and there was a sudden puff of glittering fairy dust. When it cleared, a kind-looking elderly fairy was fluttering in the air beside Jack Frost. Her wings shimmered with all the colors of the rainbow, and her snow-white hair was swept up into a neat bun.

"Good evening, Cinderfrost," she said in a low voice. "Why have you called for me?"

"Give me the perfect party outfit now!" demanded Jack Frost. "And you had better make it more beautiful than any other outfit that's ever been. Cinderfrost is going to be the most spectacular sight ever, and I want everyone else to look awful next to me!"

Rachel and Kirsty wondered if the Fairy Godmother would refuse such a rude demand, but she simply sighed and waved her wand. Suddenly Jack was wearing an ice-blue flowing cloak that glittered with thousands of tiny sequins. Long, floaty sleeves covered his arms and shoulders, and a diamond crown sparkled in his spiky hair.

Jack Frost gasped and gazed at his reflection, turning this way and that to see every inch of the beautiful outfit.

"It's my favorite color," he said at last. "This is the perfect outfit for Cinderfrost!"

The goblins around him heaved sighs of relief and several of them collapsed into a heap of clothes.

"It's about time," said one, glancing up at a clock on the wall. "You took forever to choose."

"I'm going to make a grander entrance than any princess has ever dreamed of making," Jack Frost boasted. "Everyone will be looking at me! My carriage is waiting at the back door, and then I'll ride to the front to make my entrance. They'll all be waiting in the ballroom for the most dazzling mystery guest that ever was—Cinderfrost!"

"I've got an idea," said Rachel, sounding suddenly excited. "Faith, can you disguise us as Cinderella's stepsisters?"

Faith looked uncertain.

"It would take some very special magic," she said. "I can do it, but I'll need the Fairy Godmother to help me."

Kirsty peeked into the room again. Jack was staring at his reflection, entranced. The goblins were cackling as they rolled around among the unwanted outfits. No one was looking at the Fairy Godmother.

"*Psst!*" said Kirsty. "Fairy Godmother!"

The Fairy Godmother turned and her face crinkled into a smile when she saw Kirsty. She fluttered behind the curtain to join them.

"Well, I didn't expect to meet little fairies here," she said. "What can I do for you?"

Hurriedly, the girls whispered their plan to her. She agreed right away, and, together, she and Faith waved their wands. Rachel and Kirsty stared at each other as their eyes grew narrower, their noses more pointy, and their mouths mean and tight-lipped. A few seconds later they were towering over the fairies, and they were wearing

flashy ball gowns
in ugly colors.

"You look
just like one
of the mean
girls at the
ballroom-
dancing
lesson!"
Kirsty said at once.

"You, too," Rachel replied. "Oh,
Kirsty, they must have been Cinderella's
real stepsisters. I had no idea!"

There was no time to talk about it
now. The girls pushed the curtain aside
and walked up behind Jack Frost, trying
to feel brave. Remembering how the
stepsisters had sounded, Rachel spoke in
the meanest voice she could manage.

"It's our turn to try on the glass slipper," she snapped at Jack Frost. "It's much too big for you."

"Get lost," said Jack Frost, scowling.

"But that's how our story goes," Kirsty burst out. "We have to have a chance to try on the glass slipper."

"I don't care how your story goes!" Jack Frost snapped. "I'm Cinderfrost and this is my story now, so no one is going to try on my glass slipper! Go away!"

Twilight in Fairyland

Badly disappointed that their plan hadn't worked, Rachel and Kirsty ducked back behind the curtain. Faith waved her wand and turned them back into fairies. Then she gave them a big hug.

"Thank you for trying," she said. "Jack Frost is too stubborn for words."

"We'll just have to try something else," said Rachel in a determined voice.

The Fairy Godmother gave them a gentle smile.

"I wish I could stay to help you, but someone else is calling for my help," she said. "I hope that you can stop Jack Frost from spoiling my poor Cinderella's story. She's such a sweet girl."

She held up her wand and twirled in the air, and then disappeared in a shower of silver sparkles. For a moment, Kirsty thought that she heard the sound of far-off bells. Even though she was worried about Faith's magic glass slipper, she couldn't help feeling excited. She had never met a fairy godmother before.

The space behind the curtain had grown darker—it was twilight in

Fairyland. Rachel and Kirsty looked out
of the window and were surprised to
see lots of fairies fluttering down from
the starlit sky. They were all wearing
beautiful ball gowns, and their jeweled
necklaces, tiaras, and bracelets were
glistening in the half light.

"I bet they've all been invited to the ball," said Rachel. "Jack Frost must be planning a very special evening—he doesn't normally like fairies anywhere near his castle."

"He must have wanted lots of guests, just like in the Cinderella fairy tale," said Kirsty. "Oh, of course!"

Rachel and Faith looked at her with hope in their eyes. Did she have an idea to get back the magic glass slipper?

"We should have thought about the fairy tale from the start," said Kirsty. "Do you remember how Cinderella's dress turns back to rags on the stroke of midnight?"

"Yes, and her glass slipper comes off as she runs out of the ballroom," Rachel added.

"Midnight is a very important time in this story," Kirsty went on. "Perhaps we need to see what Cinderfrost will do when the clock strikes twelve. If the glass slipper is loose, it might come off if he has to hurry."

Faith smiled—she understood exactly what Kirsty had in mind! With a wave of her wand she changed the clock on the wall so it said five minutes to twelve. She also made the glass slipper grow just a little larger. Almost at once, one of the goblins glanced up at the clock and gasped in surprise.

"Cinderfrost, look at the time!"
he squawked. "You're going to miss
the ball!"

Jack Frost let out a wail.

"Get out of my way!" he bellowed.
"I've got to make my grand entrance!"

He ran out of the room in a panic, still
wearing Faith's too-big glass slipper on
one foot and the ice-blue shoe on the
other. The fairies followed him at top
speed as he raced down the back stairs.

"Oh, please let his glass slipper fall
off!" said Rachel under her breath.

Jack stumbled as he reached the last
step, but his glass slipper stayed on. He
dashed out through the back door. An
ornate silver carriage was waiting there,
with a goblin footman standing at the
back in a green-and-gold uniform.

"Hurry up!" the footman shouted when he saw Jack Frost. "I've been out here for ages and it's freezing."

"Quiet," snapped Jack Frost.

He took a flying leap into the carriage, landing in a heap of ice-blue frills. His heel half-popped out of the magic glass slipper and the fairies darted forward, but the door slammed shut in their faces

and the carriage took off. They stared at one another in dismay.

"Let's fly ahead and hide at the entrance," said Kirsty. "I've got an idea!"

Cinderella at the Ball

While Kirsty explained her plan, they zoomed around the side of the castle toward the main entrance. There were two large statues of Jack Frost on either side of the castle door, and Rachel and Kirsty hid behind one, while Faith ducked behind the other. They were ready.

The carriage rumbled to a halt between the statues, and a goblin butler opened the castle door. The fairies could see that the entrance hall was lined with curious fairies.

Everyone stared as Jack Frost stepped out of his carriage and adjusted his tiara.

"The mystery guest has arrived!" announced the goblin butler in an important voice.

Smirking, Jack Frost moved forward
to greet his admirers. But as he stepped
between the statues . . .

"Now!" shouted Kirsty.

She, Rachel, and Faith leaped out from
their hiding place and Jack Frost jumped
high into the air in surprise. At last the
magic glass
slipper fell off
his foot and
Rachel dived
down to grab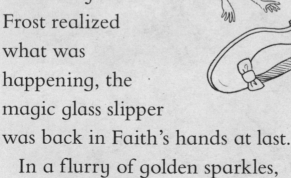
it. Before Jack
Frost realized
what was
happening, the
magic glass slipper
was back in Faith's hands at last.

In a flurry of golden sparkles,

Cinderella appeared in the castle doorway dressed in a glimmering ball gown. Her tiara sparkled in the starlight, and all the fairies cheered as she waved to them. Rachel and Kirsty cheered, too, and Cinderella saw them and gave a happy smile. Then, as everyone was

gasping at her beauty, she shimmered and faded out of sight.

"Where has she gone?" cried a disappointed fairy nearby.

"She's gone back to her fairy tale, where she belongs," said Faith, before turning to the girls with a warm smile. "And now it's time for you two to go back where you belong. Thank you for everything you've done to help me and the other Fairy Tale Fairies so far.

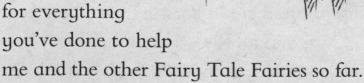

Without you, the world would be a far less magical place."

"We've loved helping—and meeting some of our favorite characters in real life," said Rachel.

"It's an honor," Kirsty added.

As Jack Frost stamped his feet and gnashed his teeth, Faith, Rachel, and Kirsty shared a big hug. Then Faith waved her wand and the girls blinked, their eyes filled with fairy dust. Seconds later, they were once again standing in the ballroom at Tiptop Castle. Rosie, the dance instructor, was waltzing around the room with Aaron.

"Cinderella's bossy stepsisters have disappeared," said Kirsty, feeling relieved.

"Yes, and all the other children are back," Rachel added, looking at the crowd of their new friends. "Come on, let's go and join in!"

They shared a wonderful lesson with their friends, with plenty of giggles along the way. By the end of it, everyone was able to waltz around the ballroom, twirling and spinning without falling over.

"Excellent!" Rosie called, clapping her hands together. "You've all picked up the steps really well. That's the end of the lesson, but I have a surprise for you. At the end of the festival, you will be using your new dancing skills at a fairy tale ball—right here in Tiptop Castle!"

There were gasps and thrilled squeals from everyone, and they all started chattering at once.

"What will we wear?"

"We need to practice more!"

"I can't wait!"

Rachel and Kirsty threw their arms around each other and jumped up and down.

"Today's just getting better and better!" said Rachel with a laugh.

The fairy tale ball was the only thing anyone could talk about for the rest of the day. That evening, the girls went to bed with a tingly feeling of anticipation.

"I wonder what the ball will be like," said Kirsty as she snuggled under the covers.

"Let's read the story of Cinderella," said Rachel, grabbing *The Fairies' Book of Fairy Tales*. Then she hopped into bed beside her best friend.

Side by side, they turned the pages until they reached Cinderella's wonderful story. All the characters were just where they belonged, together with Sleeping Beauty and Snow White. It was good to see the words and pictures back in the book as if they had never been away. They took turns to read a page at a time.

". . . and they lived happily ever after," finished Kirsty, turning the last page of the story.

Their happy smiles faded slightly when they saw that the rest of the pages were blank.

"The next story in the book should be *The Frog Princess*," said Rachel.

"I hope that we can help Rita the Frog Princess Fairy find her magic object soon," said Rachel, putting *The Fairies' Book of Fairy Tales* on Kirsty's bedside table and climbing into her own four-poster bed.

Kirsty nodded and yawned.

"It's been an exciting day, hasn't it?" she said. "I'm so glad we were able to help Faith and Cinderella."

"Me, too," said Rachel. "I wonder what adventures tomorrow will bring!"

Rachel and Kirsty found Julia's,
Eleanor's, and Faith's missing magic objects.
Now it's time for them to help

Rita
the Frog Princess Fairy!

Join their next adventure in this
special sneak peek . . .

Jack Frog?

Rachel got a closer look at the frog in Kirsty's hand.

"She's a very pretty frog," said Rachel.

"And a very lovely princess," added Rita, flying above the Frog Princess. "But unless I can get her back into her fairy tale, the story will no longer be

about her. It will be about that horrible Jack Frost!"

Rachel looked around. "He must be around here somewhere. What magic object of yours did he take?"

"My silver mixing bowl," Rita replied. "With it, I can bake the tastiest treats!"

"I can't imagine Jack Frost making anything tasty," said Kirsty.

"We must find that rascal, then," said Bertram.

"What should we do with Princess Vassilisa?" Kirsty asked, looking down at her hand.

"We can bring her to our room," suggested Rachel. "She'll be safe there."

"Good idea," said Rita. "You girls do that, and Bertram and I will start looking for Jack Frost."

"We won't be long," Rachel promised, and the girls raced back to the castle. They crossed the bridge that passed over the moat. They went through the beautiful grand entryway of the castle and climbed up the stairs to the top of one of the castle's tall towers.

RAINBOW magic™

Which Magical Fairies Have You Met?

- ☐ The Rainbow Fairies
- ☐ The Weather Fairies
- ☐ The Jewel Fairies
- ☐ The Pet Fairies
- ☐ The Dance Fairies
- ☐ The Music Fairies
- ☐ The Sports Fairies
- ☐ The Party Fairies
- ☐ The Ocean Fairies
- ☐ The Night Fairies
- ☐ The Magical Animal Fairies
- ☐ The Princess Fairies
- ☐ The Superstar Fairies
- ☐ The Fashion Fairies
- ☐ The Sugar & Spice Fairies
- ☐ The Earth Fairies
- ☐ The Magical Crafts Fairies
- ☐ The Baby Animal Rescue Fairies
- ☐ The Fairy Tale Fairies

📖 SCHOLASTIC

Find all of your favorite fairy friends at
scholastic.com/rainbowmagic

HIT entertainment

RMFAIR

Which Magical Fairies Have You Met?

- ❏ Joy the Summer Vacation Fairy
- ❏ Holly the Christmas Fairy
- ❏ Kylie the Carnival Fairy
- ❏ Stella the Star Fairy
- ❏ Shannon the Ocean Fairy
- ❏ Trixie the Halloween Fairy
- ❏ Gabriella the Snow Kingdom Fairy
- ❏ Juliet the Valentine Fairy
- ❏ Mia the Bridesmaid Fairy
- ❏ Flora the Dress-Up Fairy
- ❏ Paige the Christmas Play Fairy
- ❏ Emma the Easter Fairy
- ❏ Cara the Camp Fairy
- ❏ Destiny the Rock Star Fairy
- ❏ Belle the Birthday Fairy

- ❏ Olympia the Games Fairy
- ❏ Selena the Sleepover Fairy
- ❏ Cheryl the Christmas Tree Fairy
- ❏ Florence the Friendship Fairy
- ❏ Lindsay the Luck Fairy
- ❏ Brianna the Tooth Fairy
- ❏ Autumn the Falling Leaves Fairy
- ❏ Keira the Movie Star Fairy
- ❏ Addison the April Fool's Day Fairy
- ❏ Bailey the Babysitter Fairy
- ❏ Natalie the Christmas Stocking Fairy
- ❏ Lila and Myla the Twins Fairies
- ❏ Chelsea the Congratulations Fairy
- ❏ Carly the School Fairy
- ❏ Angelica the Angel Fairy
- ❏ Blossom the Flower Girl Fairy

3 stories in each one!

SCHOLASTIC

Find all of your favorite fairy friends at
scholastic.com/rainbowmagic

HIT entertainment

RMSPECIAL